LOBO AND THE RABBIT STEW

Written by Marcia Schwartz

Illustrated by D. B. Campbell

For Lucy, my granddaughter and *compañera* in "spinning" stories. — MS
For my kids, Thomas and Kate. — BC

Text ©2010 by Marcia Schwartz
Illustration ©2010 by D. B. Campbell

Schwartz, Marcia.

Lobo and the rabbit stew / written by Marcia Schwartz; illustrated by D. B. Campbell; —1 ed. —McHenry, IL : Raven Tree Press, 2010.

p. ; cm.

SUMMARY: Lobo the wolf attempts to outwit Bunny to put him in a stew, but Bunny outsmarts the wolf. A retelling of The Three Little Pigs.

English-only Edition
ISBN 978-1-936299-002-7 hardcover

Bilingual Edition
ISBN 978-1-936299-00-3 hardcover
ISBN 978-1-936299-01-0 paperback

Audience: pre-K to 3rd grade
Title available in English-only or bilingual English-Spanish editions

1. Fairy Tales & Folklore / Adaptations —Juvenile fiction.
2. Animals / Wolves & Coyotes—Juvenile fiction. I. Illust. Campbell, Brent. II. Title.

LCCN: 2010922814

Printed in Taiwan
10 9 8 7 6 5 4 3 2 1
First Edition

Free activities for this book are available at www.raventreepress.com

PRINTED WITH SOY INK

Raven Tree Press
A Division of Delta Systems Co., Inc.
www.raventreepress.com

As the moon rose over the canyon,
Lobo crawled from his cave.

"Oow, yeowl!" howled Lobo. "Tomorrow the moon will be full. Tomorrow I must have some rabbit stew or I will surely go crazy. I will go crazy under the full moon!"

5

Lobo's howling echoed through the canyon. Little Bunny hid under a blanket in the burrow. "Do you hear that howling?" asked Mama. "The wolf needs a tender young bunny for his rabbit stew. You must stay here in the burrow until the full moon passes." Little Bunny nodded and hid under his blanket once more.

"Tomorrow I must go down into the valley to help your grandmother pick lettuce," said Mama.

"While I am helping your grandmother, you must not leave the burrow or let anyone in. Do you understand?" she asked. "Yes," whispered Little Bunny. "Yes, I understand," he said.

Early in the morning, Mama Rabbit
hopped off to Grandmother's burrow.

Little Bunny was busy having fun. Before long, he heard a knock on the door. He remembered what Mama had said. He did not go to the door.

"Hello, my little friend," said Lobo. "I know you are in there, so let me in," he cooed.

"Go away!" shouted Little Bunny. "Mama is coming back soon and she will make a fur coat out of you!"

"Ah, don't be afraid of me, Baby. I just want to give you a treat. It is so delicious!" The wolf grinned. His mouth was watering as he thought of the rabbit stew. His mouth could taste the stew already.

"No, no, no!" yelled Little Bunny. "Go away!"

"Oh, but you will like it, my friend," said Lobo.

"Go away! I am not your friend!" said the bunny.

Lobo was getting mad. He paced above the burrow and thought, "What shall I do? The moon is almost full and I must have rabbit stew or I will surely go crazy."

Then Lobo saw the chimney. "If he won't come out on his own, I will scare him out!" he thought. Lobo returned with a snake. He dropped the snake down the chimney.

"Come out, friend, come out before Mr. Snake bites you!"

"You can't scare me," Little Bunny laughed.
"This little snake will make a good pet!"

Now Lobo was really mad. In a few hours, the moon would be full. He had to begin cooking the rabbit stew at once! Just then, he saw a barrel of cactus molasses.

"Aha!" snarled the wolf. He knew that the molasses from the cactus was very sticky and full of needles. "This will do the trick!" he cheered.

Lobo knocked the barrel over and began rolling it down the canyon toward Little Bunny's burrow. "Heh, heh!" he laughed. "Soon I'll catch you, juicy little rabbit. I shall make a most delicious stew!"

He rolled the barrel on top of the burrow and poured the gooey molasses down the chimney.

Little Bunny saw the molasses ooze
from the fireplace. He knew that the wolf
would be coming soon. He had to think quickly. He saw
a rope near the front door. He hopped over to the rope
and tied one end to the table. He held on tightly to the
other end. He waited in the burrow for Lobo.

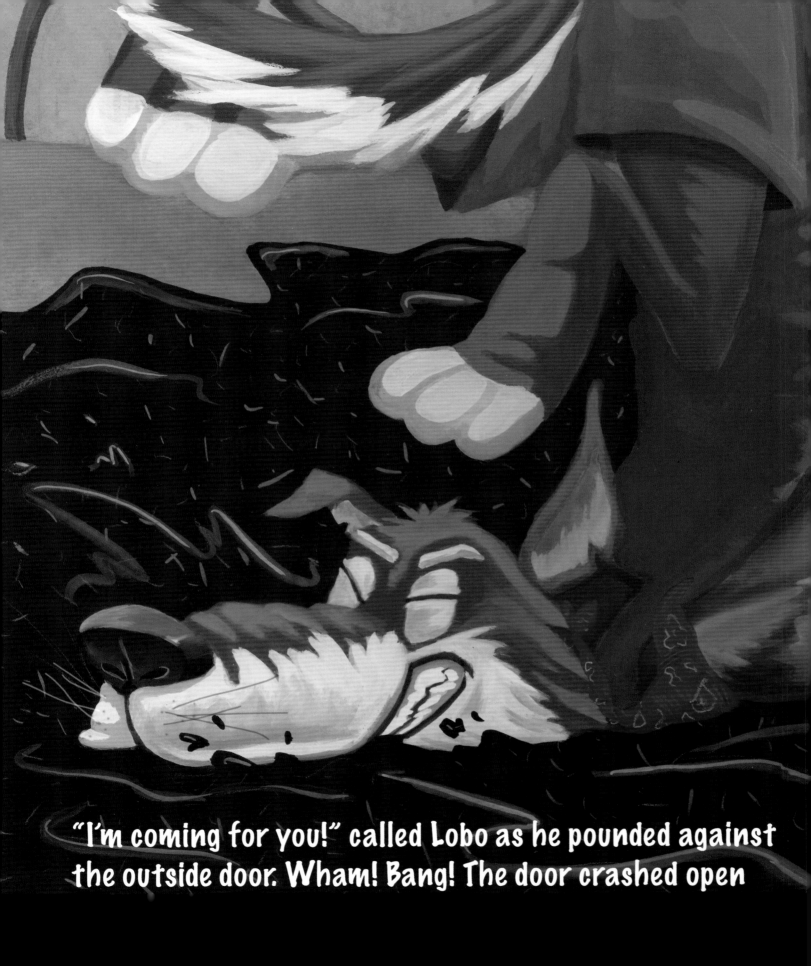

"I'm coming for you!" called Lobo as he pounded against the outside door. Wham! Bang! The door crashed open

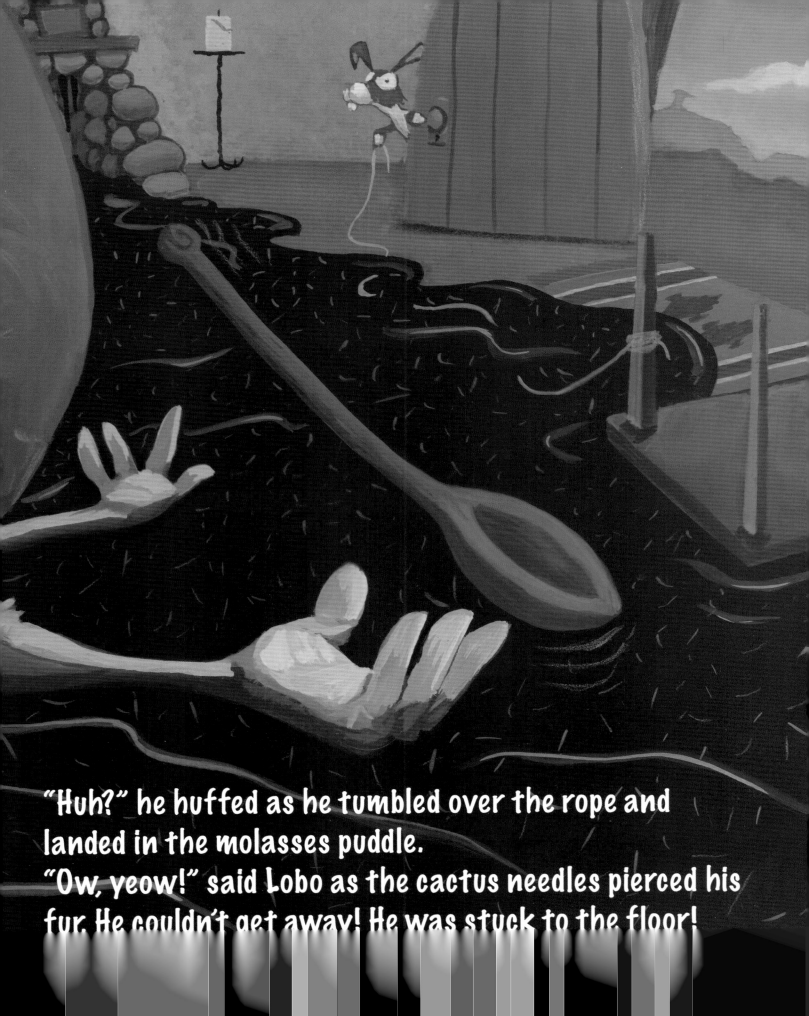

"Huh?" he huffed as he tumbled over the rope and landed in the molasses puddle.
"Ow, yeow!" said Lobo as the cactus needles pierced his fur. He couldn't get away! He was stuck to the floor!

Just then Mama returned. She saw the door open and hopped inside. "Where are you, my son?"
"Over here, Mama. I didn't leave the burrow all day just like you said. But look who came to visit."

Mama looked over to see Lobo stuck in the molasses.

"Ha! Ha! Old wolf, you didn't make a rabbit stew out of me!" called Little Bunny.

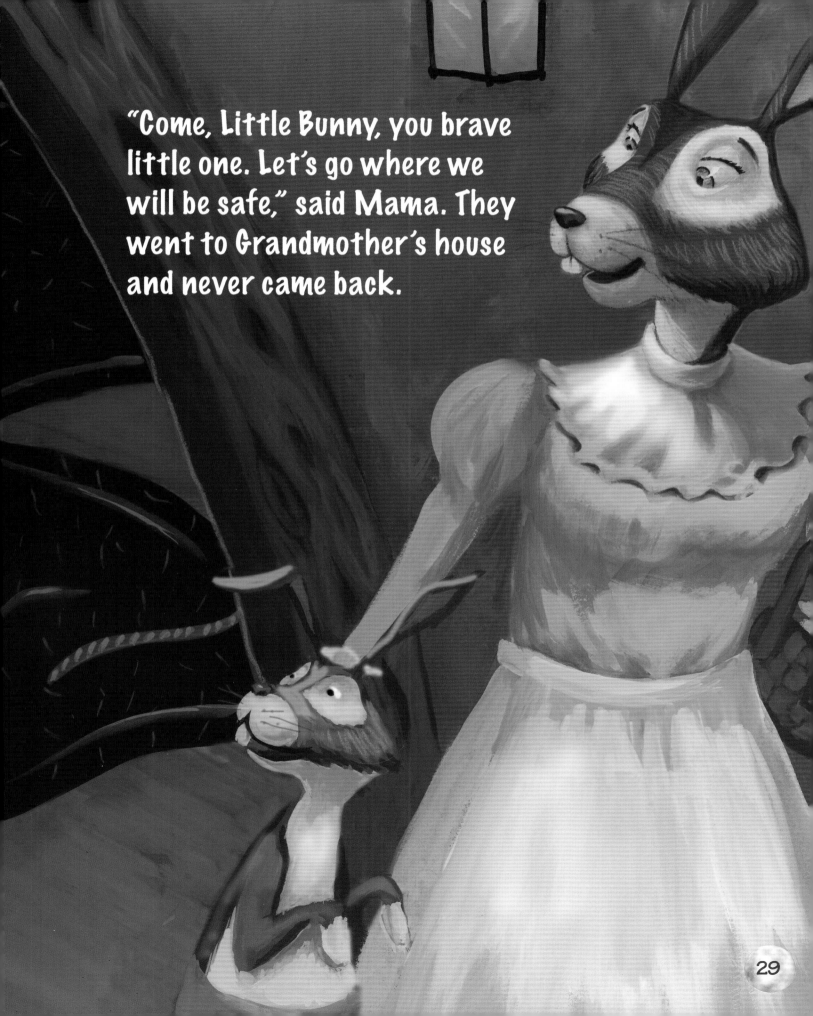

"Come, Little Bunny, you brave little one. Let's go where we will be safe," said Mama. They went to Grandmother's house and never came back.

Meanwhile, that old wolf is still plucking cactus thorns from his fur. You'll hear him howling on a clear night when the moon is full.